TAKE TARTS AS TARTS IS PASSING

by ELEANOR CLYMER

illustrated by ROY DOTY

E. P. DUTTON & CO., INC.   NEW YORK

Text copyright © 1974 by Eleanor Clymer
Illustrations copyright © 1974 by Roy Doty

LIBRARY OF CONGRESS CATALOGING IN PUBLICATION DATA

Clymer, Eleanor (Lowenton)
Take tarts as tarts is passing.

SUMMARY: Two brothers set out to make
their fortune in the world, each following
an old woman's advice differently.

I. Doty, Roy, illus.   II. Title.
PZ7.C6272Tak   [E]   73-77463   ISBN 0-525-40640-9

Published sim   la by Clarke,
Irwin & Compar   and Vancouver

Printed in   Edition

For Patty

nce there was a poor man who had two sons.

One was a hard worker and one was lazy. All the time they were growing up, people said, "Jeremiah, he's conscientious and follows orders. He'll amount to something. But Obadiah, he just wants to sit around in the shade and draw pictures and sing. He'll never get anywhere."

The two boys grew up and their father said, "There's not much for you to do in this village, boys. You'd better go out and see the world, maybe you'll make your fortune. Come back and see me in two years."

Then he sat back in his rocking chair and went to sleep.

So the boys got ready. Their father had given them each a pair of boots and a knapsack.

They were just starting out, and had not gotten past the front gate, when the old man woke up and called after them, "Wait! Don't go till you talk to Aunt Hattie!"

Aunt Hattie was a wise woman who lived in the village. She gave advice to all who wanted it and some who didn't.

Jeremiah didn't think he needed her advice. Still, he was anxious to do everything possible to make his fortune, so he hurried to Aunt Hattie's door. Obadiah followed, mainly because he liked Aunt Hattie and wanted to say good-bye to her.

They knocked at the door and Aunt Hattie came out smoking her pipe, and said, "Well, boys, what can I do for you?"

Jeremiah explained that they had come to get words of wisdom before setting out to seek their fortune.

Aunt Hattie puffed on her pipe, and then she raised her forefinger and said: "Take tarts as tarts is passing."

Then she went back inside and slammed the door.

"What does that mean?" Jeremiah asked.

"Oh, it's just her nonsense," said Obadiah, smiling at

Aunt Hattie, who was looking out at them between the curtains.

"Well, good-bye," said Jeremiah. "I must be off. I'll see you in two years."

He started down the road looking very smart in his well-polished boots and his almost-new knapsack. As he walked, he pondered: "What did Aunt Hattie's advice mean? If it was nonsense, Father wouldn't have insisted that we go to her. It's a magic spell, and if I keep my eyes open, I'll know when to use it."

Just then a wagon passed him, throwing a cloud of dust all over him. As he was crossly brushing himself off, the wagon stopped, and the driver leaned down and said, "Sorry, friend. I didn't mean to get you all dirty. Would you like a ride?"

Jeremiah looked at the wagon. It was a shabby old farm cart drawn by a dusty horse, and the back was filled with old paint cans, overalls, ladders, and I don't know what all.

Jeremiah thought, "I'll get even dirtier riding in that messy vehicle. I don't want to make a poor impression where I'm going."

"No, thanks," he called. "I'd rather walk."

He walked on until he came to the town. He thought he could get work there. He walked up one street and down another, asking everybody he met if they had a job for him. But nobody did. It was late and he was hungry and tired.

Finally an old woman took pity on him and said, "Young man, I can't spare any money, but if you'll cut some wood for me I'll give you some dinner."

Jeremiah wasn't looking for that kind of job, and he was about to refuse when he remembered Aunt Hattie's advice. Maybe this was what she meant.

"You don't by chance have any tarts, do you?" he asked.

"Tarts!" said the old woman. "No, indeed! If soup and bread aren't good enough for you, you can go elsewhere."

Jeremiah walked on. He ate some bread and cheese, which was all he had in his knapsack. He slept in a barn. At last, very rumpled and dusty, he arrived in the city.

Here too he walked up and down looking for work, when suddenly he noticed a man pushing a barrow full of pies, cakes, and fresh-baked bread. He looked to see if there were any tarts, and sure enough, there were. Apple, plum, and cherry.

"My fortune's made!" said Jeremiah, and he ran after the man and snatched a fistful in each hand.

"Stop!" shouted the man. "Hey! Police!"

A policeman came and dragged Jeremiah off to jail, and there he sat waiting for his trial. And what he thought about Aunt Hattie wasn't fit for you to hear.

Meanwhile, Obadiah, instead of starting right off on his travels, lay down to take a nap, as the afternoon was hot.

When he awoke, it was a bit cooler, so he walked down the road toward the town, when what should he see but a shabby old wagon coming toward him. It was the same man coming back at the end of the day.

The road was dusty and the wagon threw a shower of dust all over Obadiah. The driver stopped the horse and said, "Sorry, brother, I didn't mean to get you all dusty. You're the second one today. Would you like a ride?"

It didn't make much difference to Obadiah which way he went, so he said, "Thanks, why not?" And he hopped in.

They rode along, and Obadiah noticed the paint pots.

"What's all that for?" he asked.

"I'm a house painter," said the man. "But there's no work to be had around here. Tomorrow I'm going to the city and see what I can find. By the way, I could use a helper. Would you like a job?"

"Why, I don't mind," said Obadiah.

"Well, then," said the painter, whose name was Ezekiel, "come home with me. We'll have supper, go to bed, and make an early start in the morning."

"Done," said Obadiah.

The next morning, off they went to the city. Very soon they got a job painting a house. Ezekiel painted the inside and Obadiah painted the outside.

After a while he got a little tired of painting a plain color, so he painted a flower here and there on the wall.

People came along and said, "That's a new idea. Will you paint my house?"

"Why not?" said Obadiah.

In a short time he and Ezekiel had more work than they could do, and each house they painted had some flowers here and there to brighten things up.

And as he painted, Obadiah sang little songs that he made up. One of them went like this:

> Take tarts as tarts is passed along,
> And life will be a joyful song.

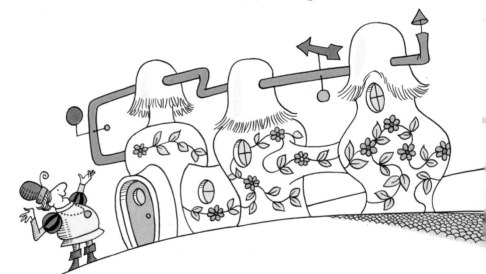

One day as he was painting and singing, along came a girl. Her hair was long and black, her feet were bare, and she carried a lute.

"That's a fine song," she said. "Would you like me to play it while you sing?"

"Why not?" said Obadiah.

So she sat down and played while Obadiah sang and painted.

And so time went by.

One day a man came along and listened a while.

Then he said, "I have a boat that goes up and down the river, and people come on board and go for a sail in the moonlight, or in the sunshine, and I'd like very much to have a young couple like you to play and sing for them. Will you come?"

Obadiah and the girl (her name was Emmeline) looked at each other and then at Ezekiel.

Then Obadiah said, "We'd like mighty well to go, but we don't want to leave Ezekiel."

But Ezekiel said, "That's all right, you've brought me so much trade that I'm very well off now, and if you should decide to leave, I'll not stand in your way, though I'll miss you."

So Obadiah and Emmeline went off with the boatman, and for many days they sailed up and down the river playing and singing and having a lovely time.

One day Obadiah said, "I'd like to go on singing and playing this way forever."

"Then maybe we should be married," said Emmeline.

"Why not?" said Obadiah.

So the captain of the boat married them, which is something a captain is allowed to do.

But he said, "I'd like you to stay on with me, for so many people want to sail on my boat and hear your music that I can hardly find room for them all."

Obadiah looked at Emmeline and said, "Why not? We'll be glad to stay."

So they stayed, and after a while they had a little baby daughter, whom they named Lizzie.

Well, one day Obadiah said, "You know, it's two years now since I left home, and I promised to go and report to my father about whether I made my fortune or not. The only trouble is, I haven't made a fortune, though I expect Jeremiah has."

"Well, we ought to go and see your old father anyway," said Emmeline. "I'm sure he'd like to see little Lizzie."

So the boatman steered his boat to the dock nearest the village where Obadiah lived. They said good-bye to the boatman, who was so sorry to see them go that he almost cried. But they promised to come back some time.

Then the boatman said, "Wait!" And he ran down into the hold and came back with presents for them. For Emmeline he had a pair of shoes, for little Lizzie he had a doll, and for Obadiah, as luck would have it, he had a box of tarts, a little stale but still good. They were all things that passengers had left behind.

So they walked along till they came to the village, and Obadiah led the way to his father's house.

The old man was still sitting in his rocking chair.

"Hello, Father," said Obadiah. "I'm back, and this is my wife, Emmeline, and this is our daughter, Lizzie."

"Well, I'm glad to see you all," said the old man. "Have you made your fortune?"

"Well, no," said Obadiah, "but we really don't need one. We're happy as we are. But what about Jeremiah? Isn't he here?"

"Why, there he comes now," said the old man.

And sure enough, down the road they saw a man trudging along, dusty and miserable-looking.

It was Jeremiah, all right, and when he reached the house he sat down on the top step and wiped his face.

Emmeline went to him and said, "Oh, Jeremiah, I'm your new sister, and I'm so glad to see you. Here, have a glass of lemonade and one of these delicious tarts."

"Tarts!" said Jeremiah. "Take them away! They're the cause of all my trouble. Them and Aunt Hattie."

And at that Obadiah began to laugh. "Oh, Aunt Hattie!" he said. "I told you it was all nonsense."

And he picked up the baby and swung her around until she laughed too.

ELEANOR CLYMER is the author of more than forty books for children. Her books for young readers include *The Big Pile of Dirt* and *My Brother Stevie* (both Holt) and *We Lived in the Almont, Me and the Eggman,* and *The House on the Mountain.* Mrs. Clymer grew up in New York City and now lives in Katonah, New York.

ROY DOTY has been twice voted Illustrator of the Year by the National Cartoonist Society. His illustrations and cartoons appear in numerous magazines and advertisements. His first picture book was *Girls Can Be Anything* by Norma Klein. He lives in Stamford, Connecticut, with his wife, a writer, and their four children.

The illustrations are done in black line with color overlays. The display type is Souvenir and the text type is Granjon. The book was printed by offset.